THE RELUCTANT BRIDE

OREGON TRAIL SERIES
MAIL ORDER BRIDES
BOOK #1

KATIE WYATT

Royce Cardiff Publishing House

UNITED STATES OF AMERICA

Royce Cardiff Publishing House
428 Childers Street
Pensacola, FL 32534
www.KatieWyattBooks.com

The Reluctant Bride Book 1 -- 1st edition
PAPERBACK ISBN 9781549841125

Dear reader, this book is dedicated to YOU.

We would like to personally thank you for buying this book and supporting us.

Your letters, emails and reviews mean the world to us and give every book we write special meaning.

Would you like Would you like a FREE book.

Go to http://katiewyattbooks.com/vipreadersgroup/

CONTENTS

OREGON TRAIL SERIES
MAIL ORDER BRIDES

THE RELUCTANT BRIDE

A Personal Word from Katie

This story was inspired by reader Maria. This is book one in a four-book series (Oregon Trail). It starts with Betsy, an independent attractive and a teaser of a young lady. She has a lot to learn about life, and if she's not careful, she just might herself pushing up daisies. She gets herself into some deep trouble by eyeing men, she should not be looking at. This is her story of her trials, tribulations and unexpected adventurous in her life and the genuine meaning of love.

Get ready to enjoy a good laugh with this spirited bride. Betsy will need every ounce of pluck and determination to tame her new family as well as the Oregon Trail.

<u>Oregon Trail Series</u>

Book 1 The Reluctant Bride

Book 2 Step Children

Book 3 The Torn Heart

Book 4 The Road Home

I sure hope you enjoy this tale as much as I do.

Thank you for being a loyal reader and also to Maria!

Katie

CHAPTER ONE

Christmas Day 1849, Raleigh, North Carolina

If I hadn't had too many glasses of wine and Charles Bishop hadn't been so darned charming, I would never have ended up in dire straits. Well, probably not. But the wine was flowing at the Hamiltons' annual Christmas cotillion and I was determined to enjoy myself. I'd had to wear my maroon silk taffeta gown again, since I didn't have the money for a new dress. Still, with its nipped-in waist and low-cut bodice, it never failed to capture the attention of at least a few of the men in the room. The Hamiltons weren't exactly high society, which was the only reason that I was invited. There was an abundance of food and the wine, while not the best, was at least plentiful.

I had danced with half a dozen young men, all the while flirting with Charles Bishop from across the room with my eyes. No matter what event I attended, I always tried to find one man who became my secret target. If I could get his attention and keep it for most of the evening, I won. It was a silly game, but always rather fun.

This time, my target was Charles Bishop. You might think less of me, but he was married. I know, how dare I do it? Before you shake your finger at me too hard, you need to know that his wife was an absolute harpy. She was pinched and bitter and a hopeless prude. I don't know how she married the likes of Charles Bishop, who was quite the opposite. In fact, he was quite delectable.

So, I was quite pleased to find that the hand on my arm while I was waiting for another glass of wine belonged to none other than Mr. Bishop himself. He nodded his head towards the door to the ballroom and I had to suppress a victorious smile as I glanced around before sneaking after him into the hallway and then into the darkened study.

"You wanted a word with me," I teased once we were tucked inside the shadows.

His voice was mellow and deep and sent tingles up my spine. "I want more than just a word, Miss Bradley."

My heart began to gallop. "On what topic, sir? I can't imagine what we have to discuss."

Charles' hand came out of the shadows, slipped around my waist, and firmly guided me closer to him. "With the way you look tonight, I don't think we need to waste time talking."

This was the point where my good sense swam through the alcohol which was making my brain feel fuzzy. It screamed at me to reconsider the wisdom of this particular scene and to hurry back to the party. Unfortunately, my ego was quite inflated by the wine and Charles' words. It recalled the snub his wife had most recently given me and my good sense was stuffed back down into the depths of my soul. What harm was there in exchanging a few flirtatious remarks with this man in a darkened room where we were all alone? I most certainly enjoyed flirting with good-looking men. In fact, I prided myself on my ability to kiss and still escape with my virtue intact. Of course, I wouldn't go so far as to kiss a married man, but I couldn't stop myself from wondering what it would be like to be kissed by Charles Bishop.

I turned to smile at him coyly but found myself off balance thanks, no doubt, to the wine. Without thinking, I reached out and grabbed Charles' arm to steady myself. Gallantly, he took hold of my arm, throwing his other hand around my waist to keep me from falling, and the two of us bent dangerously towards the floor. At the last minute, Charles was able to find his balance and I rested in his arms, head spinning.

Suddenly the door flew open and light from a lantern filled the room. Mrs. Amelia Bishop entered the room wearing a dull gray silk dress that reached her throat and an expression of horror.

"Charles! Get away from that floozy," Amelia hissed. Behind her, two of her cronies entered the room wearing similarly boring gowns and equally shocked faces.

Charles was only too quick to pull away from me,

which left me dizzily reaching for a nearby chair. I widened my eyes and tried not to giggle at the scene. Amelia Bishop deserved to find her husband in the arms of another woman. Being discovered in such an embrace was not going to help my reputation any, but it was immensely satisfying.

"Betsy Bradley, I should have known." She crossed her arms and glared at me. "Most women leave other women's husbands alone. Only a hussy like you would seduce a married man."

I lifted a finger, fully intending to tell her that Charles had come quite willingly, no seduction required. However, my brain and mouth seemed unable to synchronize themselves and I was only able to widen my eyes and mouth wordlessly.

"Drunk, too," one of the other women sneered. "Disgusting."

They soon stormed off, Charles in tow. I was starting to feel sleepy and so decided that the party was over for me. I collected my wrap and walked a crooked line all the way back to the room that I rented in the women's boarding house. By the time I was dressed in my nightgown, hairpins dropped carelessly on the dressing table, dress in a pile on the floor, the scene in the study was fading away to little more than a vague haze.

In fact, the next morning I didn't give it another thought. I spent most of the day nursing a terrible headache and feeling mildly guilty for not attending church on Christmas the day before. The bookstore where I worked was owned by a British immigrant who felt that Boxing Day should be observed in the New World. Since it meant that I wasn't required to work for two days in a row, I happily agreed every time he broached the topic. It was a good thing I had the day off from work, since every loud noise made me moan and hold my head.

The day after, however, I awoke feeling mostly better. My encounter with Charles Bishop was coming back in hazy bits and pieces and I felt rather superior about the whole thing. However, once I arrived at the store, I learned that I had made a terrible mistake.

***

Amelia Bishop, as I came to learn, was dear friends with the wife of the shop owner who employed me. Not only were they friends, they owed Amelia some money for helping them to start the bookshop. Apparently, Amelia decided that revenge was needed and told her friend that, unless I was fired, the loan would be recalled immediately.

That was how I came to be standing in front of my employer, a Mr. Nigel Peters, and his wife. Mr. Peters was quite apologetic. His wife was staring daggers at me and clutching her husband's arm possessively. Did she really think that I was going to try to seduce her middle-aged, paunchy, bewhiskered husband? Really. I did have some standards.

"I'm so sorry, Miss Bradley, but we'll have to let you

go," Mr. Peters said, wringing his hands. "We just can't afford to keep you on at this time."

"And good riddance," his wife spat. "You won't find work in this town. Not respectable work, that is."

I pushed down the urge to explain myself and beg forgiveness. Instead, I accepted the wages that were due to me, lifted my nose in the air, and gave Mr. Peters a lingering kiss on the cheek and overly fond arm pat, just for the fun of watching his wife bristle. Then I turned sharply and walked out the door and into the street where I stood, not knowing what I was going to do.

Unfortunately, I wasn't terribly qualified to do much of anything. I was an adequate shop assistant, but I wasn't a hard worker or meticulous accountant. The bookshop had been ideal, since Mr. Peters was easily managed. A breathy laugh and fond pat of his arm and he was a perfect lamb. I spent most of my time doing a poor job of dusting the shelves and reading every novel I could get my hands on. It was a lucky thing that Mrs. Peters hadn't gotten wind of my work ethic sooner.

I sighed. There was nothing for it. I would simply have to go from door to door asking for work. I turned and made my way to the first shop along the way, which happened to be a stationery shop. If I could sell books, I was confident I could sell paper and the like.

Patting any wayward strands of hair back into place, I picked up my skirts and stepped into the shop. I took in the tidy display in the window and the boxes lining the shelves. It was a small building and I began to doubt the likelihood of finding a job here before I even made it to the counter, where I was greeted by a smiling, round woman.

"How may I help you, my dear?" she beamed at me.

I dug out my most charming smile and said, "I'm looking for work. Are you, by any chance, hiring?"

"I don't know." The shopkeeper wrung her hands and began to sweat. "My husband makes those sorts of decisions and he's not in at the moment. Would you mind leaving your name?"

"Certainly," I continued, smiling. "I'm Betsy Bradley."

Her happy expression spluttered and was snuffed out. "I'm sorry, Miss Bradley, but we don't need any additional help at this time."

I blinked at her slowly. The sudden change of temperament caught me off guard. Feeling stung, I turned and made my way quickly back to the street. What an odd encounter. I ran over the brief exchange in my mind and couldn't think what had gone wrong. Of course, in such a small shop, it was unlikely that the owners would need additional help. Still, the proprietor had seemed interested until she heard my name.

"Amelia Bishop!" I hissed, coming to a complete stop in the middle of the street. My fists bunched at my sides and I felt my stomach sinking even as my ire rose like a molten tidal wave. Was it possible that Amelia Bishop had put a black mark on my name?

By the end of the next hour, I knew I'd guessed correctly. The cobbler seemed as though he might hire me until I reluctantly gave my name. The milliner's wife knew me on sight and refused me entry to the store. Even the hardware shop refused to hire me, despite a solid ten minutes of flirting with the cute young man who worked the counter. I retired to my room at the boarding house that night with steam coming out of my ears.

"How can Amelia Bishop keep me from working?" I fumed to my next-door neighbor, Mary Ann.

"You did kiss her husband," Mary Ann pointed out as she filed her fingernails. "I guess you picked the wrong woman to tangle with."

I threw myself into the chair in her room and threw up my hands. "I keep telling you: I didn't kiss him! Of course, it's not as though she kisses him. A man whose wife keeps him happy isn't one to go flirt with another woman. Besides, why would anyone want to kiss Amelia Bishop? She's so sour; it's probably like kissing a lemon."

Mary Ann smirked before pointing her file at me. "If you can't find work soon, Betsy, you're up the creek without a paddle."

"I'll find a job. She can't influence every business owner in Raleigh." I crossed my arms, determined not to give in.

But by the end of the week, I had to admit that I was thoroughly stymied. Somehow Amelia Bishop had coerced, convinced, or threatened everyone in town who might have hired me. I couldn't be a governess, a shop girl, a seamstress, or even a kitchen maid. My only option was to work in a saloon, and even I had some standards.

***

I had exhausted every lead I could find by the first of January and had almost exhausted my savings. Rent was paid up through the end of the month and my landlady, Mrs. Burton, allowed me to work in the kitchen to pay for my meals. I wasn't desperate yet, but I wasn't far off.

As I washed dishes on New Year's Day, I grumbled to myself. Most people who find themselves in any kind of trouble head to the refuge of their parents for help. Mary Ann's family lived in the country somewhere nearby and, while she swore she'd never go back there, she knew that if things got bad, had she had a safety net. Unfortunately, I had no such luxury. My parents had died when I was a girl. Papa had gone first in a hunting accident and Mama and I moved in with her mother. Then Mama grew sick and was gone almost overnight. I was left in the care of my austere grandmother, who found me most trying.

She refused to call me Betsy. To her, I was Elizabeth, though it wasn't really my name at all. I grew up hearing her sigh and say, "Quiet, Elizabeth, you're bringing on my headache." Home was never a place where I felt safe or wanted. So, I made a home with my friends. At school, I was quick to endear myself to a group of girls who were always at the center of any scandal. Together, we honed our flirting skills, teased the younger children, and did whatever we could to keep the schoolmaster off topic so he forgot to give us homework. Once we grew up, we each went our separate ways and I found a new group of friends.

Grandmother died when I was sixteen and I was left her meager estate. Once the funeral home took its cut and the bills were paid, I wasn't left with much to live on. I cheerfully moved to Mrs. Burton's boarding house and found work where I could. I fell in with a merry group of shop girls and we made certain to have as much fun as possible whenever we weren't at work.

Over the past two years, I'd been content. Now, however, I wished I had a family. I even wished Grandmother was alive so I would have somewhere to go when my money ran out. It would have been worth enduring her sighs of long suffering if it meant I didn't have to think about what I would do next for a few hours.

The very worst part of the whole fiasco was that my girlfriends were starting to keep me at arms' length. They weren't as friendly as they had once been. When I'd mentioned attending the New Year's Eve gala, they'd exchanged nervous glances.

"I don't know if I'll be attending," Dorothy said, refusing to meet my eyes.

"My mother wants me to come home for the evening," Jane smiled weakly. "She's such a bore."

"I don't really have anything to wear." Helen fiddled with her bracelet before changing the subject.

In the end, they went without me. I spent the evening sitting in my room and thoroughly regretting ever flirting Charles Bishop. A wicked part of me wished I had kissed him, though my conscience was quick to shake its finger at that thought. I was stewing in my own juices, and a sorry sight indeed.

That was how, on January 2nd, I found myself entering the office of a Mr. Harold Wainwright, who advertised a mail order bride service.

CHAPTER TWO

Mr. Wainwright was surprisingly fussy for such a large man. He would have looked right in overalls, with a pitchfork in hand. Seeing him in the small, tidy office was an immediate shock. For one thing, he almost filled the room, spilling out over his desk, his elbows touching the filing cabinet on his right and the windowsill on his left. But his hair was neatly pomaded, his vest tasteful, and his fingers were carefully manicured.

So when he spoke, his smooth, well-chosen words seemed to fit. "Good day, miss. How may I be of service?"

I put on my full smile and tried not to give offense. "I might be in a position of needing to find a husband."

"Please, have a seat." He stood as much as the cramped space allowed and gestured to the only other piece of furniture in the room. "Let me tell you more about how this process will go."

To be completely honest, I didn't listen much to what he said. I was too busy wrestling with myself. It felt absurd to be here even considering marrying a stranger. Were things really this bad? There was always the chance that I might still find work or even a potential suitor here in Raleigh. But, what if I couldn't? My savings were quickly dwindling. It was already too late to move to a new town. I didn't have enough money for a boarding house, or even a train ticket. My situation was grim and I probably should have paid more attention to Mr. Wainwright's spiel.

"Once you have selected a gentleman, you will sign a contract agreeing to marry him. In exchange, he will pay your train ticket West, where you will be immediately married. Should either party not go through with the wedding, the other is within his or her rights to sue for breach of promise."

I supposed this was meant to be a comfort. But I didn't want a husband, just a train ticket out of North Carolina. Looked like I wouldn't be able to get one without the other through this company.

"Do you have any questions?" Mr. Wainwright was asking.

"What if the man isn't what he said he would be? What if he says he's a banker but he's gone bankrupt? What if he's old? How do I know that the man I'm promising to marry is who he says he is?" I was more interested in taking some of the polish out of Mr. Wainwright, rather than being genuinely curious.

However, the man across from me smiled calmly and went smoothly into the next part of his speech. "Our firm has taken special precautions to eliminate any untruthfulness. Our agents meet with the men who apply, take their specifics personally, and require all money upfront. Of course, there are no guarantees in life, but we take steps to ensure that our brides are safe and well cared for. In fact, our agents often speak with local ministers or priests to learn if the men who apply are regular church attenders."

Oh, goody. I wasn't sure that I wanted a groom whose church attendance was spotless. I managed a weak smile. "How soon would I be expected to leave?"

"Within a week, usually," Mr. Wainwright beamed. "Once the contract is signed, I will telegraph the agency who took the gentleman's application and he will be notified. We then purchase your train ticket and you are ready to depart."

I swallowed hard. A week didn't sound like much time at all. Of course, I did have the money to pay for another week's stay in the boarding house, though not much beyond. The time frames lined up neatly, darn it.

"Can I have some time to consider?" I asked as my fingers found their way to one of my earbobs and began to fiddle with it.

"Of course you can. Take all the time you need. Why don't we look through some files and see if anyone jumps out at you?" Without waiting for my answer, Mr. Wainwright wrestled a drawer open and selected a few files from inside. He licked a finger, then began to dramatically turn the pages within. "Ah, here's a good candidate."

In all, I was shown four potential husbands. They were mostly from the Midwest, though there was one in Montana. The thought of lonely Montana winters made him easy to eliminate. Of the remaining three, one was older than fifty, one was a widowed farmer, and one lived with his mother.

I felt my lip curl and my heart sink as I looked over the pages. There was no way I would marry an old man. I pushed that file back towards Mr. Wainwright. A widower? A mother-in-law living with her son? Which was the lesser of two evils? Lifting a tremulous hand, I slowly pushed back the man living with his mother, then picked up the remaining file.

His name was James Tucker and he lived in Oklahoma. He was a farmer whose wife had died two years ago. He lived on a farm in the northeastern part of the state and was only a few months away from owning the land outright. That was all the information I had on which to base my decision.

"I'll need some time to think," I said. Suddenly, I needed to be out of the cramped room.

"Naturally. I'll hold this file for two days for you, but I cannot promise to wait much longer than that." Mr. Wainwright seemed to be sneaking a threat into his kind words.

I bid him good day and all but ran out the door. Once outside in the street, I gulped in huge breaths. Good Lord, had I seriously been contemplating marrying a stranger and moving to Oklahoma, of all places? I started down the street, hoping that each step would diminish the memory of that rash meeting.

By the time I turned onto the street my boarding house was on, I was pretending that I was feeling better about my circumstances. However, when my name was called, I was so lost in thought that I almost didn't hear. A hand reached out and touched my elbow and only then did it register that someone had been calling me.

I pulled myself out of my reverie and blinked up at a tall, attractive young man. "Mr. Bertram! I didn't see you there." My hand flew to my bosom and I laughed prettily.

Frank Bertram laughed in response and struck a pose that showed off his physique to advantage. "You looked as though your thoughts were a thousand miles away."

Was that how far Oklahoma was from here? If so, it was a good guess. I smiled becomingly. "What are you doing over on this part of town?"

"I was hoping to run into you, actually," he flirted. "Is there any chance I can convince you to take pity on a poor lawyer and have supper with me?"

My smile grew. Perhaps this was the last-minute savior I'd been hoping for. "I would be delighted. Would you allow me to change my dress first?"

"Of course." Frank held out his elbow, which I took, and led the way to Mrs. Burton's boarding house, where I scurried upstairs and changed into my Sunday best. There was no time to improve my hairstyle. Besides, I wanted to strike just the right note with Frank. It had to be a mix between appearing to like him and not hoping for too much from him. I didn't want to seem desperate (though I was), but also wanted to seem interested, should he want to begin a courtship.

We walked to a nearby restaurant. It wasn't one of the fancier ones, though the food was good. Our flirtations grew bolder as the meal progressed and, by the time we started the walk back to my residence, I was enjoying myself thoroughly. Surely Frank had every intention of asking to call again. There would be no need for me to marry a stranger or move to Godforsaken Oklahoma.

I held Frank's arm and pressed myself against his side. "Thank you ever so much for dinner, Mr. Bertram. I've had a terrible week and this was just the lift my weary spirit needed."

Frank's steps slowed and he said, "I heard about what happened at the Hamiltons' party. I bet Amelia Bishop was irate when she caught you in bed with Charles!" He laughed a coarse laugh that made me pull back from his arm a bit.

"She didn't catch us in bed," I explained moodily. "We were only flirting. In fact, when she walked in, we weren't even doing that."

Frank shot me a look that clearly expressed his doubts on that score before tugging me into the shadowed alley between two office buildings.

"What are you doing?" I demanded in a whisper. I knew the sort of women who spent time in dark alleys and the last thing I needed was to be mistaken for one.

Before he answered, Frank swung me around, pressing my back against the wall. I only had a moment to worry that my dress would be damaged before he was kissing my neck. He pulled back and said huskily, "I know your landlady is a bit of an old prude. I thought we could say good night out here."

It was a bad idea. I agree with you. There was no way that allowing Frank Bertram to kiss me was going to do anything for my reputation. Still, it might mean that he intended to continue to call on me. Besides that, I did so enjoy kissing attractive men.

We went on in that manner for several minutes. I was thinking that it was about time to stem Frank's ardor when he groaned and pressed himself against me, his hands unbuttoning the front of my dress.

"Stop that!" I ordered, trying to push him away.

He grinned wolfishly at me and moved to kiss me again. I slapped him across the face with enough force to stop him without actually hurting him and he stepped back, hand to his cheek.

"What was that for?" he demanded.

My hands went to my hips and I pulled myself up to my full five feet and two inches. "What do you think? I'm not the sort of girl who allows a man to paw her in a dark alley, Frank Bertram."

"Is that what you think?" He moved his jaw back and forth experimentally. "For your information, Miss High and Mighty, that's exactly what we were just doing. And from what the fellows around town are saying, this isn't the first time you've done that sort of thing."

My gasp of shock didn't slow him down. Frank narrowed his eyes at me and went on. "In fact, I've talked to half a dozen men who claim to have bedded you. There's a line forming for when you finally take up work at the saloon. I figured I'd try and get a taste for free, before you start charging."

The words left my mouth. I stood there feeling as though I'd been punched in the gut. With no viable defense, I lifted my chin, sucked in my tears, and left the alley before I started sobbing. As it was, I barely made it into my room before I sank onto the floor, my back to the door, and gave in to my absolute despair.

***

There was really nothing left to be done. In the morning, I slunk back to Mr. Wainwright's office and signed the contract to marry James Tucker. Before I knew it, the arrangements were made and the train ticket was purchased. My final days in Raleigh were quiet and uneventful. Rather than meet with all my friends and demand that we celebrate my departure, I hid in my room. All I wanted was to leave town without a fuss. Besides, it felt that everyone was avoiding me, now that I'd run my reputation to complete ruin.

In the end, I had only Mary Ann and Mrs. Burton to bid goodbye. Mary Ann was kind enough to pull out her hankie and dab at her eyes in a show of sorrow at our parting. Mrs. Burton looked faintly relieved to have me out of her house and no longer as a blight on her business.

I was a subdued woman as the train pulled out of the station. Everything that was familiar was rolling away and the unknown was rushing at me at the breakneck speed of 40 miles per hour. I'd never ridden on a train before, I realized glumly. My grandmother had read somewhere that the human brain would explode if it traveled above thirty-five miles per hour and had always warned against the dangers of the train. Though I miserably wiped away a tear once we reached full speed, I still managed to roll my eyes at her old-fashioned worries.

I might have felt relief at leaving all my mistakes behind, but there was too much fear of the unknown to allow my spirits to rise much. The first hour of the trip, for that matter, I spent listing all my faults and shortcomings. By the second hour, I'd moved on to promising to stop flirting with men and be a good wife, even if James Tucker turned out to be a hateful drunkard who beat me. I was picturing myself as a martyr for marriage when a man in a sharp herringbone traveling suit settled in the seat across from me.

"You are much too lovely to be so sad," he cooed, "if you'll forgive my effrontery, that is."

We hadn't been properly introduced. A lady in my circumstances would never allow herself to enter into a conversation with a man who was not in her acquaintance. It was also true that a lady wouldn't be traveling alone, let alone fleeing her home due to her risqué behavior. I wasn't sure what the paragon of virtue that I hoped to become would do in this situation. The deflated, discouraged woman that I already was knew exactly what to do, however.

"Of course," I smiled demurely. Even if I spoke with this stranger, I could still be ladylike, couldn't I? After all, it wasn't a sin to speak to a man on a train.

"My name is Herbert Lyle and I am a traveling salesman. I have ridden the rails all over this fine country of ours and I always take the time to speak with young ladies who are traveling alone. It isn't safe, you know." He leaned forward, the very picture of sincerity.

"My grandmother always warned me of that very fact." I held out my gloved hand. "I'm Betsy Bradley."

"Ahem, *Miss* Bradley?" Mr. Lyle took my fingers gently and bowed over them as his eyes eagerly awaited my response.

"For now," I said with a flirtatious smile. Darn it. I had only made it a few minutes before my resolution to behave crumbled. "I'm on my way to meet my intended husband."

Mr. Lyle sat back and crossed his legs. He was attractive in a slick, carefully planned sort of way. I felt like I was being watched by a sly predator who was waiting to pounce. I didn't have many salesmen in my general acquaintance, but I supposed this must be what they were all like.

"Forgive me for saying so, Miss Bradley, but how is it that your fiancé is willing to allow you to travel alone over what must be a large distance?" He appeared concerned, but something around the edges crackled with a suppressed energy that made his words tingle with some unspoken other meaning lying just beneath.

It was the tiniest bit dangerous. And, unfortunately, I loved dangerous men.

"Our marriage was arranged through a broker." I felt embarrassed to say the words and fiddled with the drawstring of my purse.

Mr. Lyle's eyes widened and he shook his head slowly. "What sort of buffoons were in your last town to allow a woman like you to get away? If you had been a single woman in my city, I would have paid suit the moment your father allowed it."

I ducked my head and smiled shyly, as though his compliment was making me blush. There was no way on earth I was about to tell him the truth of why I had agreed to become a mail order bride.

The train jostled around a bend and Mr. Lyle took advantage of the momentum to shift from the seat across from me into the one directly beside me. He was sitting very close for a man I'd just met. My brow furrowed as I tried to decide whether or not I should admonish him and send him back across the way.

"I know that you've already arranged to marry this stranger, but I can tell that you have reservations." His eyes were a warm brown and so close to mine. His knee was only a hair's breadth from mine.

I blinked up into his face, eyes wide, the picture of innocence. "It is strange to contemplate marrying a man I've never met."

Mr. Lyle tutted. "Of course it is." He glanced around, as though checking for listeners. "I have an idea that might help you considerably." He leaned forward and said quietly, "I know a woman in Chicago who is always looking out for pretty young ladies. She runs a tea house, you see, and needs to find hostesses. Do you know about tea houses?"

I shook my head, half mesmerized by his closeness and half by his intense gaze.

"Oh, they are a modern marvel! Refined ladies who find themselves in difficult financial circumstances have taken to opening tea houses in large cities across the nation. Gentlemen are able to stop in for a cup of tea and some company from the elegant hostesses. Many business owners have taken to inviting clients they wish to impress to such eateries. They are all the rage." He sat back a bit and let me mull this news over.

"How do you know that this lady is hiring at the moment?" I asked, unable to quench the excitement that perked up inside me.

He waved a hand as though it was a silly question. "The trouble with tea houses is that the hostesses are young ladies of a certain caliber and it caters to gentlemen. The young ladies are rarely employed for more than a month before one of their patrons makes an offer of marriage. I believe one of the state's senators is married to a lady he met at just such an establishment."

My head was spinning. What a fantastic opportunity! To think that I could escape from the clutches of James Tucker and find a work in a tea house where I might find a husband who would be handsome and wealthy! I had a dozen questions for Mr. Lyle and turned to start my inquiry when a tall soldier sat in the seat across from us.

"Please excuse me, miss," he said. "This man means you nothing but harm."

I gasped and leaned away from Mr. Lyle. Could it be true?

"You know nothing of the sort, young man," Mr. Lyle laughed. "Now, please, let me continue my discussion with this poor girl."

The soldier shook his very handsome head. "I know who you are. You are a confidence man who preys on young women traveling alone. There have been reports of your kind lately."

"I shall stay and speak to this young lady as long as she allows it." Mr. Lyle looked at me with a winning smile. The danger that had crackled around the edges of his façade flared.

"No," I said, lifting a hand to my throat. "I don't care to continue this discussion."

He snarled and pulled himself to his feet, shooting a hateful look at the soldier, before oozing his way down the car to find another victim.

As soon as Mr. Lyle was out of the car, the soldier moved to the seat next to me.

"I don't know how to thank you," I said breathlessly.

"I'm just glad I walked past when I did. My name is Simon Hart and I'm a corporal in the United States Army. I'd be pleased to offer you my protection as long as we share this train."

My heart fluttered. This was positively just like something that would happen in a novel. And Corporal Hart was as handsome as any hero in a book could ever be. He was tall and broad shouldered. His hair was a rich mahogany and waved nicely, though it was cut in a military style. His eyes were a lovely gray and were set off to perfection by his tanned skin. I thought his nose and high cheekbones were a bit aristocratic.

"I'd be ever so grateful, Corporal Hart." I fluttered my eyelashes at him.

We settled back in our seats and began the usual conversation that new acquaintances inevitably embark upon. I learned that he was the youngest of five and had been in the army for several years. He'd only just made corporal and the change in rank required a change in location as well. Thus, he was traveling from the east coast to Fort Laramie in Wyoming Territory. He kept me entertained with stories of the terrible sergeant he'd served under in his early days as a soldier, as well as a detailed description of the dog his family had owned growing up and how much he missed the old rascal.

With each turn of the wheel, I found myself drawn further under Simon's spell. I was quite mesmerized by the time the morning had passed. Most men I'd met I knew only well enough to flirt with. I couldn't remember a man who I knew so much about. That level of intimacy made me feel as though our lives were slowly being intertwined. Flirting with him was fun, of course, but our long, winding conversation sprouted a fondness for him that was very new and exciting.

CHAPTER THREE

By the time we made our way to the dining car for supper, my conscience was starting to make weak attempts at getting my attention. I'd spent hours talking with Simon and had managed to avoid mentioning James Tucker. Simon was quite gentlemanly towards me and never once said or did anything he shouldn't. After my last encounter with a male suitor, this was much appreciated. I did lose track of what he was saying sometimes as I focused on his perfect lips and thought about what it would be like to kiss them. Our arms did brush from time to time, but that was all the physical contact we had.

I sat across the small table from him and looked over the menu. Naturally, I'd been on many dinner dates with men over the years. A few of them had been quite promising, though nothing much had ever developed. Sitting across from Simon Hart, however, was by far the most romantic of the lot. There was something delicious about having been saved by his gallantry that set the evening off to perfection.

The steward took our orders and we turned our attention back on each other.

"Simon," I began. We'd progressed to calling each other by our first names sometime in mid-afternoon. "Do you have an understanding with a young lady back home?"

It was a brazen thing to say. My grandmother would have been shocked.

He raised an eyebrow and smiled coyly at me. "That's a leading question. Why do you ask?"

"As much as I appreciate your protection, I would hate for you to feel that you were being untrue to your girl by having dinner with me." I said it as innocently as possible, though I rested my chin on my hand as I spoke and smiled back just as coyly.

"Of course. What a noble thought." Simon leaned forward and rested his arms on the table. Our faces were less than a foot apart. "I do not have a girl back home. Though I have found many women I admired, I have yet to find one I wanted to commit myself to."

It was my turn to raise an eyebrow. Under the table, his foot found mine and came to rest touching it. My heart turned over a little. Now was most definitely the time to come clean.

I cleared my throat. "I see. Well, you might as well know that I am going to Oklahoma to marry a man I've never met."

Simon's face fell a little. He looked away as he gathered his thoughts. Finally, he turned back to me with a brave smile. "While I'm sorry to hear that you are affianced, I must admit that I am hardly in a position to offer you more than my friendship at this time."

He'd handled that hurdle well. Unfortunately, that made it all the much harder. I nodded and took a roll from the basket and began to butter it. Hopefully, my disappointment wouldn't be noticeable in the shaky lamp light that tried to illuminate the car.

"How is it that a woman of your caliber is marrying a stranger?" He followed my lead and chose a roll for himself.

I sighed. It was hard to believe, but I actually wanted to tell Simon the truth about my stupid actions in Raleigh. After all, even if he was disgusted by me, we were only going to share the train another day or two and then never have to see each other again.

"I've become a terrible flirt over the past few years," I began. By the time my confession was finished, Simon's eyebrows were halfway up to his hairline and he had a barely-suppressed grin twitching on his face. I rolled my eyes. "You probably think I'm a wanton woman now."

He burst out laughing and the people at the tables nearby shot us disapproving glares. Simon covered his mouth with his napkin until he had his giggles under control.

I had turned prickly during this outburst. Being laughed at was never something I tolerated well. I picked up my fork and worked away at my supper, roundly ignoring him.

"I'm sorry," he croaked finally. "You poor thing! Why is it that spirited young women always get the bad end of the stick?"

I looked at him, trying to measure his sincerity. "I believe it's because dull women marry attractive men and resent the freedom of those of us who dare to live life."

"I agree. I can just imagine the look on this Mrs. Bishop's face when she caught you alone with her husband. I wish I'd been there to see it." He started laughing again, but this time I found that I didn't mind it so much. "Good for you for teaching her a lesson. I can't bear wives who refuse to see their husbands as men who need to be cared for."

"I can't either," I sighed. "How can women agree to marry a man and then never want to kiss him again? I'm sure you'll think less of me for saying so, but I've kissed my fair share of men and they never want to stop. I don't know how a woman could believe that she's married to someone who doesn't want to kiss her."

Simon's eyebrow raised again. "I've kissed a fair number of women, so you'll get no condemnation from me. I've appreciated every one of those girls who were willing to shuck propriety. I can imagine that you're a master of the art yourself."

Something warm and tingly uncurled itself in my stomach. Oh, what I wouldn't give to find a shadowy corner where I could show him just how much I knew about kissing! But I was on my way to be married. Shouldn't that mean that I stayed out of such corners with fellows who weren't my husband?

"I hope James Tucker appreciates my skill." I slid my reminder in primly.

Simon's eyes grew dark and my skin prickled. "Perhaps you'll have to get in just a bit more practice before you promise to kiss only him for the rest of your life."

I let that thought soak into my mind: kissing one man for the rest of my life. What a dreary prospect that was. Surely there wouldn't be any harm in passing a few pleasant minutes in the arms of this devastatingly handsome soldier? James would never need to know about it.

"I suppose you're going to be off fighting Indians soon and risking your life." I pretended to be thinking it over.

"Oh, yes," Simon played along. "In fact, I could lose my life any day now. Would you deny me the comfort of one last kiss?"

We sat looking at each other for one more moment before getting to our feet and making our way down the aisle and out the door between cars. There were a fair number of people in the next car, so we continued on until we found an empty storage car that was filled with wooden crates.

The light coming in through the doors at either end of the car cast everything into shadows. Simon reached for me and was like a huge, hulking figure looming out of the dark. I looked up at him and gasped in delight. Then his lips were on mine. I forgot all about the discomfort of the wooden crates poking me in the back. I forgot about my promises to behave myself. I forgot all about James Tucker. The only thing I knew was the feel of Simon's lips on mine, the taste of his breath as we pulled apart, and the scratchiness of his wool coat under my hand.

I truly believe that we were in that car for at least an hour. Time lost all meaning. My muscles grew sore from standing so that I wasn't leaning back into the boxes around me. Only then did I pull away from Simon's growing passion and suggest that we go back to our seats.

He cleared his throat before kissing my hand and said, "You should go first. If anyone sees us leaving this car together, it might cause a scandal."

I leaned in for one more ardent kiss before pulling away and opening the door. Once out on the step, I gratefully let the cold night air cool my heated cheeks. That had been one of the best hours of my life; there was no doubt about it. As I made my way back up two cars to my seat, I found myself wondering, how in the world was I going to let Simon Hart go so that I could marry someone else?

***

I woke up on the morning that the train would arrive in my destination and sat in my seat looking over at where Simon still slumped against the window. Despite having spent three nights sleeping sitting upright, not having a bath or a change of clothes since I left Raleigh, and knowing that I was rumpled and probably starting to smell, I couldn't remember ever feeling so happy.

I'd spent almost every minute in Simon's company since he rescued me that first day. We had discussed important topics, lighter subjects, and even sat in silence. There was something amazing about being able to be with a person for so long and not grow tired of him. Any time he got up to visit the lavatory or to stretch his legs, I missed him. Whenever he returned, my heart would leap in my chest. Sometimes when he looked at me and smiled, I became lost in simply enjoying gazing at his handsome face. There was a crackle of electricity between us that I'd never experienced before. And when we kissed, I thought I would swoon.

Part of me wanted him to take my hand and swear his undying love to me and beg me to come with him to Fort Laramie, where we would never again be apart. It would be terribly romantic if such a thing occurred. But another part of me wanted to keep this short pocket of time as perfect as it had been up to now and not sully it with mundane reality. After I married James Tucker, I could remember Simon Hart fondly as I went about my dull chores. I even had a very exciting, if not particularly practical, fantasy in which James was cruel and Simon

appeared, fought him to the death, and carried me
away.

No matter what the next few hours brought, I woke
up that morning with a full heart. It was equal
parts hope, resignation, worry, and the need to live
each remaining moment with Simon so that I would
never forget it. Taking care not to wake him, I
inched past and made my way to the ladies' room,
where I washed myself as well as possible, combed
and repinned my hair, and did whatever I could to
make myself presentable.

By the time I returned to my seat, Simon was
awake. He took a turn in the men's room and then
we made our way to the dining car for breakfast.

We ordered our food and then sat sipping our coffee
and looking out the window, somehow unable to
meet each other's eyes. It was hard to even know
what to say. Asking him how he slept would be stiff
and forced. All our small talk felt like it was only
filling the time before we would have to say things
we'd never forget.

I was glad when our plates were delivered and we
could turn our attention to eating. By then I knew
that Simon liked his coffee black, his eggs runny,
and butter on his toast. He had very nice table
manners, too. I enjoyed watching him use his
cutlery with precision.

"What is it you will be doing at Fort Laramie?" I
asked. We'd talked about many things, but few of
them were about the future. Suddenly I regretted

not knowing what was ahead for him. I wanted to be able to picture Simon going about his life while I was going about mine.

He took a sip of his coffee then said, "I'm a part of the cavalry. I believe that I will be assigned to a unit and we will conduct whatever missions our commanding officer decides we need to perform. There's been some threat from Indians in the area. I expect to spend time maintaining peace."

"Is it dangerous?"

"I imagine it can be." He nodded slowly. "Any time we have to deal with people who have a different opinion of how things should be done, we risk stirring up a bit of a fight. I hope that the settlers in the area will be able to live without fear, now that fresh recruits are arriving."

My heart sighed a little. He was so brave and noble. I smiled at him and ate the last of my sausage.

"Do you think you'll be getting married today?" Simon asked, startling me into choking on my last bite.

I coughed as delicately as I could while my mind frantically tried to form an answer to his question. Once I was able to speak again, I stalled a little longer by taking a long drink from my water glass. Finally, I could put it off no longer.

"I hadn't really considered when the wedding would take place." I looked out the window at the bare trees, patiently waiting out the winter. "I don't know if James will want to be married right away." What a frightening thought that was!

Simon reached across the table and put his large, tanned hand over mine. I was able to allow my eyes to meet his then. "He's a very lucky man to be able to claim you for a bride."

Tears rushed into my eyes. Darn it, I wasn't going to cry! I needed Simon to think that I was brave and strong and unafraid of this new adventure. Unfortunately, I felt small and scared and I didn't want him to ever leave me.

I pressed my lips together and blinked the tears away.

He leaned forward urgently. "Betsy, if I could, I would take you with me to Fort Laramie and save you from marrying James Tucker."

"You would?" I whispered, voice quavering, heart leaping.

He smiled tenderly. "If I wasn't sure that I would get in terrible trouble, not to mention subjecting you to life in the army barracks, I would have proposed to you the first night we were on the train."

My heart positively sang. No matter how much men seemed to enjoy my company, not one had ever gotten so close to proposing. It was as though I was always on the edge of the dance floor, always waiting to be asked to dance and always being passed over for someone else who was superior to me in a way I never could understand. True, this wasn't an actual proposal, but I was going to count it as such in my memory.

"James would have grounds to sue me if we ran away together." I tried to sound as though I didn't take his words too seriously.

"I could face a court-martial." His smile was fading. "I suppose I'll have to be content with the memory of you and these past few days together. They've been some of the best of my life, Betsy. Thoughts of you will keep me warm many a cold night over the next years."

I was lost. I tried to keep my crying quiet and pat at my tears with my handkerchief as quickly as they came. Once I could speak again, I said, "I feel the same about you, Simon. I don't know why we met when we could never have a future."

He slowly shook his head and swallowed hard. "It's so unfair."

It was. We sat in silence for a while, holding hands and feeling glum.

"May I write to you?" Simon finally asked. "I want to know that you're keeping well and that James is treating you right."

"Of course you can write," I blurted. "I don't know my address, though."

"Perhaps you could send me a letter once you're settled in. Just address it to me at the fort and I'll get it."

"You'll write back?" I asked, unable to resist a bit of coy flirtation.

His eyes met mine and the intensity there took my breath away. "Within the hour."

And then it was time to return to our seats to gather my things and prepare to leave. The conductor came through announcing our imminent arrival in Guthrie, which was my destination. I sat next to Simon, our hands clutched as we felt each last moment together slip away. The farms outside the window began to grow closer together, and soon the edges of a town appeared.

Once Guthrie was announced and the train slowed, I looked up at Simon and was filled with sadness at everything that we would never get to do.

"I should go," I whispered, sure my heart was breaking.

"I'll come with you and wait until James Tucker arrives." Simon made to stand.

"No," I replied quickly. "I don't think I could go off with him if you were standing with me."

He searched my face, then looked away as though he couldn't bear to say goodbye. "I'll walk you to the door."

I agreed and stood to collect my things before leading the way down the aisle. Simon loped behind me and I was grateful to put off our separation another minute. When we reached the door, however, Simon took my arm and pointed his chin back towards the end of the train. Curious, I followed him as he led me through the other passenger cars. Once we arrived in the dark car full of crates, I knew that Simon wanted a more private goodbye, and I was so very glad he did.

We didn't speak for several minutes, too busy with other things. Finally, I knew I couldn't put it off any farther.

"Goodbye, Simon," I whispered.

He dug in his pocket for a moment and then asked, "May I have a lock of your hair?"

It was such a romantic thing to say that I quickly acquiesced. He drew out a pocket knife and I loosened a strand of my dark hair so that he could cut off a few inches. Once done, he lifted the lock to his lips and kissed it.

"I'll never forget you, Betsy Bradley, and if our paths ever cross again, I won't let you go."

I threw myself back into his arms for another kiss and then tore myself away, afraid that I wouldn't be able to leave him if I waited even another second. And then I was standing on the platform, unable to see anything through my tears. Why did I have such rotten luck? The one man who actually met me and wanted me, I couldn't marry. It was terribly tempting to turn and run back to the train and board again. Never mind that I would have to stay in an army barracks. Never mind that my trunk was being dropped on the platform even as I stood there crying. Never mind James Tucker and his lawsuit.

I turned and forced myself to walk to the waiting room and find a seat. I dabbed at my eyes with my already-wet handkerchief and tried not to draw anyone's attention. For a rare moment in my life, I wanted to be invisible. The sound of the train's whistle blowing brought on a fresh wave of tears and when it chugged away from the platform, I was sure I'd never felt so small and alone in my life.

After an hour of waiting, though, I had myself pulled together somewhat. I missed Simon desperately, but I felt ready to face James Tucker and our new life together. Again, I was picturing myself as a martyr, though this time one more on the lines of Juliet. I would bravely marry a stranger and begin my life as a farm wife. I would not miss my friends back home and a life of enjoying parties and suppers with handsome admirers. I would be faithful to James and never kiss another man again. Oh, woe.

"Excuse me," a male voice interrupted my journey to the depths of despair.

I looked up and saw the silhouette of a well-built man blocking the light from the door. "Yes?" I asked as I raised a hand to block the sunlight from the open door.

"My name is James Tucker. Are you Miss Bradley?"

"Yes, I am." I got to my feet and held out my hand. "I'm pleased to meet you, Mr. Tucker."

He took my hand and pressed it gently. I was still unable to discern what he looked like exactly, so I focused on his hand, which was broad and rough, the skin cracked around his nails. This was the hand of a man who worked hard. I couldn't decide whether or not I found it appealing and knew I would have to reserve judgment about him until I had more information.

"Shall we go to the wagon?" He turned and led the way out of the waiting area before I could respond.

Eager to see him properly, I followed without a fuss. In the bright winter light, I blinked until my eyes adjusted. Then I looked around for where my husband-to-be was wrestling my small trunk into the back of a wagon. As I made my way to him, I took in his broad, well-muscled shoulders and arms. James Tucker was far more attractive than I'd dared to hope. I could only see his face in profile, but it was very pleasant indeed. He had thick, curling blond hair that was cut short on the sides and was combed back on top. He kept a close-shaved beard, though no mustache. His eyebrows were straight and stood guard over deep set, serious eyes. Without a further word exchanged, I knew him to be serious, hardworking, and not one to break the rules. Darn it.

This wasn't the sort of fellow I usually found attractive, but I knew other boring women loved this sort of man. So what was it that had kept James Tucker from finding a bride?

The answer became apparent a moment later.

"Ready to go?" he asked me brusquely. I nodded and he helped me climb up into the wagon. Then James turned and called, "Let's go!"

I looked around, confused. Who was he calling to? The horses?

To my horror, three small blurs shot out from behind the buildings nearby and James lifted them into the back of the wagon.

"Miss Bradley, these are my children, Emma, Lucy, and Joseph. Children, this is Miss Bradley. She's going to be your new mother."

I stared at the three wiggling, dirt-smeared creatures in shock.

James swung himself into the seat beside me, then cracked the reins and said, "I've warned the preacher that we'll soon arrive to be married, if that suits you."

It didn't seem to matter much if it suited me or not. I was thoroughly and completely stuck. I dared one more peek over my shoulder. Two of the children were pretty small and had settled back, chattering and pointing. The oldest girl caught me looking at her, crossed her arms over her chest, and shot me a look that could kill.

What had I gotten myself into?

To continue enjoying Book#2 "The Step Children" Please go visit us at

https://www.amazon.com/Step-Children-Oregon-

Trail-Book-ebook/dp/B0735JDC44/

In addition, there are some high value mega box sets available below for your reading pleasure. As always, they are FREE for Kindle Unlimited.

Katie Wyatt 25 Book Mega Box Set Complete Series

Katie Wyatt 26 Book Mega Box Set

Katie Wyatt 27 Book Mega Box Set

Katie Wyatt My Brothers and the Golden Key Series

Katie Wyatt Box Set Sweet Frontier Cowboys Novel 1-3

Katie Wyatt Box Set Sweet Frontier Cowboys Novel 13-15

Kat Carson Mary and Abigail Complete Series Novels 1-2

Katie Wyatt 3 Book Box Set Nuns and Cowboys Series

Katie Wyatt Love of a Child Complete Series

Katie Wyatt 8 Book Collection Complete Series

Thank you so much for reading my book. I sincerely hope you enjoyed every bit reading it. I had fun creating it and will surely create more.

Your positive reviews are very helpful to other reader, it only takes a few moments. They can be left at Amazon https://www.amazon.com/Katie-Wyatt/e/B011IN7AF0

If you would like to know about all my new releases and have the opportunity to get free books, make sure you sign up for my newsletter and
http://katiewyattbooks.com/vipreadersgroup/

ABOUT THE AUTHOR

Katie Wyatt is 25% American Sioux Indian. Born and raised in Arizona, she has traveled and camped extensively through California, Arizona, Nevada, Mexico, and New Mexico. Looking at the incredible night sky and the giant Saguaro cacti, she has dreamed of what it would be like to live in the early pioneer times.

Spending time with a relative of the great Wyatt Earp, also named Wyatt Earp, Katie was mesmerized and inspired by the stories he told of bygone times. This historical interest in the old West became the inspiration for her Western romance novels.

Her books are a mixture of actual historical facts and events mixed with action and humor, challenges and adventures. The characters in Katie's clean romance novels draw from her own experiences and are so real that they almost jump off the pages. You feel like you're walking beside them through all the ups and downs of their lives. As the stories unfold, you'll find yourself both laughing and crying. The endings will never fail to leave you feeling warm inside.

Made in the USA
Monee, IL
03 July 2022